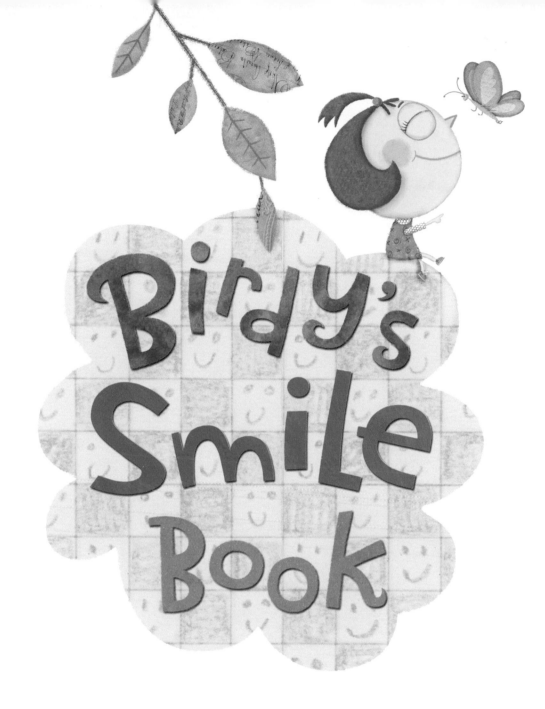

Birdy's Smile Book

Laurie Keller

Christy Ottaviano Books

Henry Holt and Company ✽ New York

Hi! I'm **Birdy**
and this is my dog,
French Fry.

And THIS is my smile.

I heard an old saying—
"Let a smile be your umbrella."
I tried that once.

I got soaking wet.

So I made up a NEW saying—
"Let an umbrella be your umbrella."

It's important to have a good umbrella.

But it's MORE IMPORTANT to have a good smile.

I smile at myself **every** morning.

I think
the
first
person
you see
each day
should
look
HAPPY
to see you.

BESIDES...

it warms me up to greet the world with a smile!

Smiles make people **Happy!**

I try to smile at **everyone** I see. And most of the time they smile back!

Mmmmr mhrrm mmhhrr mmrrmr mhhrm mmmrm mrmmmhrm.

He said he can't smile because his mouth is rusted shut!

I'm not sure why, but CHEESE makes people happy, too.
Whenever someone takes a picture they say,

Say, "Cheese!"

Then everyone says

CHEESE!

and they smile!

Aw. shucks.

I like that.
If I were food, I'd be cheese.

I just feel so happy!

It's because of the cheese!

I like how everyone's smile is different.

Lucy Lollipop's smile is small **and** sweet.

Chip Zipperman's smile is BIG and shiny. *

April Crumpet's smile curls up on the ends—just like her hair.

Principal Price's smile dips under one side of his nose . . .

. . . and pops back out on the other side!

The Grizzle Twins' grins aren't **EXACTLY** the same—
but I can't quite figure out the difference.

And Troy McSwooney's
smile is . . .

OH, RIGHT!

My best friend, Pearl, can make HER smile reach all the way up and touch her glasses!

Ta-da!

I can't see my grandpa's smile because his **mustache** is SOOOo **big** it covers his whole mouth!

But somehow I can always tell when he's SMILING.

Grandpa says my smile can light up a room.

I wish it could **CLEAN** up a room, too.

Smiling is easy. You can smile when you:

Say the alphabet
Climb a tree
Brush your teeth
Stand on your head
Build a snowman
Take out the garbage
Ride a zebra
Cross your eyes and hop on one foot
Blow your nose
Act like a monkey
Eat broccoli

Everyone looks better with a smile
(even if they don't have very good teeth).

Presidential Teeth

I wish George Washington, the first president
of the United States, had known that.

Poor George.

His teeth were SO BAD that they all fell out except for one! He wore fake teeth made of hippopotamus ivory and cow teeth. YUCK! Maybe that's why he didn't smile much.

If he were here today I would say to him:

PLEASE SMILE, GEORGE. I don't care if your teeth ARE disgusting, I just want you to SMILE, silly!

Then if he STILL didn't, I'd pin him down and tickle him! THAT would get him smiling. George would like that, I bet.

A smile can make
a NOT-SO-GOOD thing seem . . .
NOT-SO-BAD.

I like it when smiles get **SO SMILEY** that they burst into **LAUGHS!**

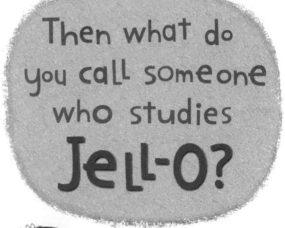

It's easy to smile when I feel

glad.

But sometimes I feel

bad

or

mad

or

sad

and don't feel like smiling.

My smile is smart though.
It knows when to leave me alone . . .

. . . and when to come back.

Once, after I found her lost cat, TOPSY, Mrs. Flapjack smiled so hard that tears came out.

That smile must have HURT!

Mom said those were tears of joy and that sometimes people get SO HAPPY that they cry.

BREAKING NEWS!

The Department of Facial Expressions has just confirmed that SMILING IS GOOD FOR YOUR HEALTH. They say the simple act of smiling releases natural chemicals called ENDORPHINS into the body, which make people feel HAPPY, which make people feel RELAXED, which make people HEALTHIER. I hope they will also find that smiling promotes hair growth, but so far there have been no such reports.

I'm happy that smiling is good for us but I'm **MOSTLY** happy about the **endorphins** being released!

Smiles are CONTAGIOUS.
That means they spread fast, like
chicken pox, but they're not as itchy.

You can say THAT again!

Just think...
if I
smile at
SOMEONE...

who
smiles
at
SOMEONE...

who
smiles
at
SOMEONE...

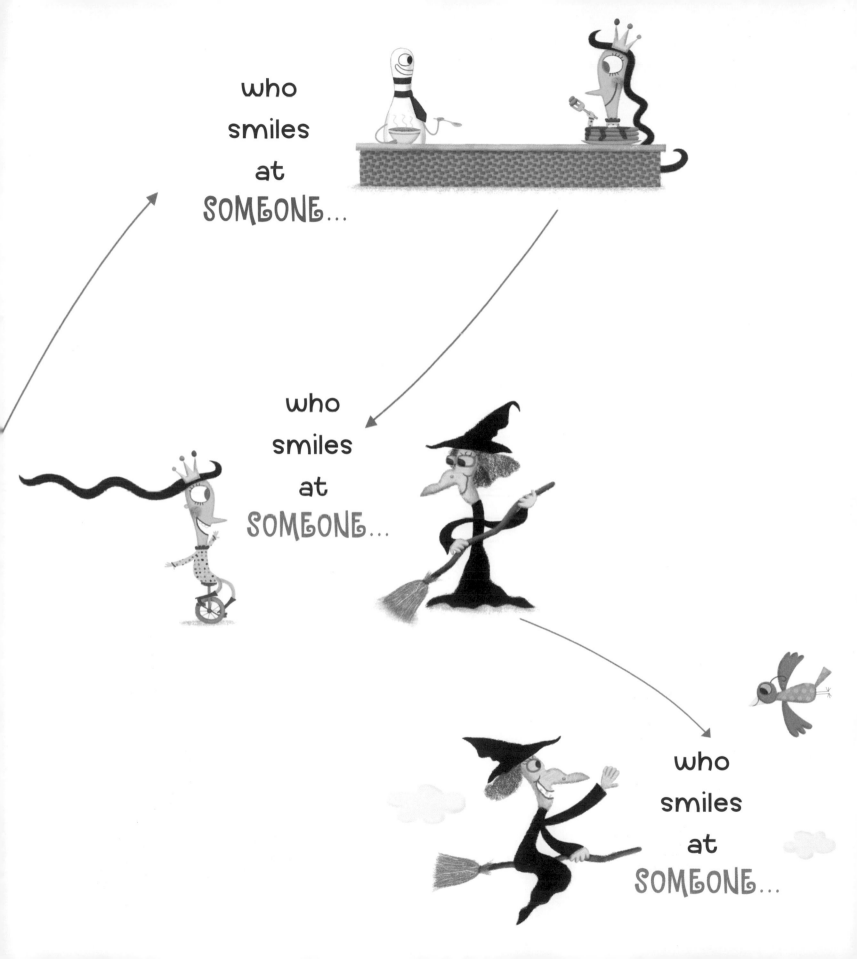

who
smiles
at
SOMEONE...

who
smiles
at
SOMEONE...

who
smiles
at
SOMEONE...

. . . there's no telling **HOW FAR** my smile might travel!

Hey, I just thought of something!

If I can get a smile all the way to **Timbuktu,** then maybe I can get one to ...

...the moon!